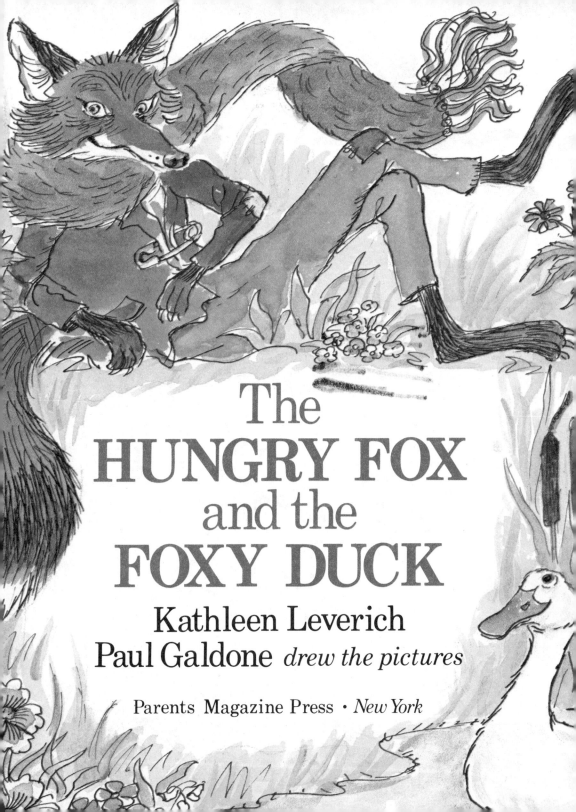

The
HUNGRY FOX
and the
FOXY DUCK

Kathleen Leverich
Paul Galdone *drew the pictures*

Parents Magazine Press · *New York*

For BXN   K.L.

For Barbara Francis   P.G.

Text copyright © 1978 by Kathleen Leverich
Illustrations copyright © 1978 by Paul Galdone
All rights reserved.
Printed in the United States of America
10 9 8 7 6 5 4

Library of Congress Cataloging in Publication Data
Leverich, Kathleen.   The hungry fox and the foxy duck.

   SUMMARY: A fox in pursuit of a wise little duck
learns the hard way why she lives exactly where she does.
[1. Ducks—Fiction. 2. Foxes—Fiction]
I. Galdone, Paul. II. Title.
PZ7.L5744Du   [E]   78-11215
ISBN 0-8193-0987-7   ISBN 0-8193-0988-5 lib. bdg.

Not far from here there once lived a very wise little duck.

This little duck lived
on a pond in a field
with a fence all around.

All day long,
the little duck would
sun herself and swim.

Life was peaceful
on the pond in the field
with the fence all around.

One morning the little duck
saw a hungry red fox.
The fox stood on the bank
of the pond.

"Come and have breakfast with me,"
Fox called to Duck.
Duck looked at Fox.

"This fox is hungry,"
she thought to herself.
"He looks hungry for ducks."

The little duck thought quickly.
"How can we eat breakfast
without a table?" she asked.
"Wait right there," called Fox.
"I will get a table."

Fox ran across the field.
He ran under the fence.
He ran through the forest
until he came to a
woodcutter's hut.
Fox looked inside.
No one was home, but a
little table stood by the window.

"Woodcutter won't miss
this table," thought Fox.
And he stole the table.

Back ran the fox to
the pond in the field
with the fence all around.

Fox could almost smell
the roast duck he
would have for supper.

The little duck was swimming
in the middle of the pond.
"Here is a table," called Fox.
"Come and have breakfast
with me, Duck."

"You are too late,"
called the little duck.
"I ate while you were gone.
Now it is almost lunch time."

"Well then," called Fox.
"Come have lunch with me."
Fox was very hungry for roast duck
after all that running.

The little duck thought quickly.
"How can we eat lunch
without plates and cups?"
she asked.

"Wait right there," called Fox.
"I will get plates and cups."

Fox ran across the field.
He ran under the fence.
He ran down the road
until he came to a
potter's shed.
The potter was not there,
but Fox saw a pile of
plates and cups.

"Potter will not miss these,"
thought Fox. And he stole two
plates and two cups.

Back ran the fox to
the pond in the field
with the fence all around.
Fox could almost taste
the roast duck he
would have for supper.

The little duck was
swimming in the middle
of the pond.

"Here are the plates
and cups," called Fox.
"Come have lunch with me, Duck."

"You are too late,"
called the little duck.
"I ate while you were gone.
Now it is almost supper time."

"It is indeed," said Fox,
and he licked his chops.
"Come have supper with me."
Fox was tired and cranky
and hungry for roast duck
after all that running.

The little duck thought quickly.
"How can we eat without
a tablecloth?" she asked.

"If I get a tablecloth, *then*
will you eat supper with me?"
demanded Fox.

"Yes," said the little duck.
"Wait right there," called Fox.
"I will get a tablecloth."

Fox ran across the field.
He ran under the fence.
He ran along the river
until he came to a
washer woman's house.

The washer woman was
not there, but a bright red
tablecloth hung on the
clothesline.

"Washer woman will not
miss this," thought Fox.
And he stole the tablecloth.
Back ran the fox to
the pond in the field
with the fence all around.
Fox could hardly wait
for the first bite of
his roast duck supper.

The little duck was
swimming in the middle
of the pond.

"Here is a tablecloth," called Fox.
"Come for supper, Duck."

"Hold up the tablecloth, Fox,"
called the wise little duck.
"I do not think it is big enough."

"It is big enough," called Fox. And he waved the red tablecloth to prove it.

Then Fox learned why
the field had a fence
all around it.

Fox never came back.
Duck lived happily.
Life was peaceful on
the pond in the field
with the fence all around
to keep the bull in.

About the Author

Kathleen Leverich was born and grew up in Greenwich, Connecticut, but now lives in Boston, where she devotes all her time to writing. She has been an editor of *Cricket Magazine* and is a former children's book editor with a leading publishing house. *The Hungry Fox and the Foxy Duck* is her first book.

About the Artist

Twice runner-up for the Caldecott Medal, Paul Galdone, that grand master of folktale art, has illustrated over 275 picture books, including several which he wrote as well. Born in Budapest, he came to New York as a teenager where he studied painting under Guy Pène du Bois, Louis Bouché and George Grosz. He and his wife divide their time between their homes in New City, New York, and Tunbridge, Vermont. *The Hungry Fox and the Foxy Duck* is the first book Mr. Galdone has illustrated for Parents Magazine Press.